The Ghosts of CREAKIE HALL in Star Spooks

Karen Wallace
and Tony Ross

Catnip

To Nick 'n' Jane

CATNIP BOOKS
Published by Catnip Publishing Ltd
14 Greville Street
London EC1N 8SB

This edition first published 2011

First published by Hamish Hamilton Ltd 1998
1 3 5 7 9 10 8 6 4 2

Text copyright © Karen Wallace, 1998
Illustrations copyright © Tony Ross, 1998
The moral rights of the author and illustrator have
been asserted

A CIP catalogue record for this book is available from
the British Library.

ISBN 978-1-84647-124-7

Printed in Poland

www.catnippublishing.co.uk

CHAPTER 1

MIASMA BOGEY-MANDEVILLE pushed open the attic window and rested her ghostly silver arms on the ledge. A warm breeze ruffled her knee-length orange hair. Spring had finally come to Creakie Hall.

Miasma smiled and gazed down at her favourite things. Bullfrog Lake was bubbling with bullfrogs. The maze was turning thick and green and looking more like a prison than ever. Miasma never tired of watching spring come to Creakie Hall even though more than three hundred springs had come and gone since she and Marmaduke had first moved up to the attic.

'Shiver me timbers!' croaked Marmaduke behind her. 'Where be that lunatic on the lawnmower?'

Miasma turned and smiled at him. Over the years, in between their poker games, Marmaduke had taken up various hobbies. Pirates were his latest. He was obsessed by them. He read books about them. He painted pictures of them. He insisted on eating what they ate. This was where Miasma lost patience – weevily biscuits and rum were not her idea of a tasty snack. Even Cromwell, their cat, had been roped in. These days he sat on Marmaduke's shoulder with a patch over one eye.

Marmaduke stood up and clanked across the room to the window.

He could barely walk what with the swords and blunderbusses that hung about him. 'Where be the varmint?' he cried, scanning the lawn with his telescope.

'Marmaduke,' murmured Miasma, reprovingly, 'you mustn't talk about Osbert Codseye like that. Anyway, why are you so interested?'

Osbert Codseye was the gardener. His lawnmower was his pride and joy and he drove it with the elegance and ceremony of a maharaja riding an elephant. Indeed, on a hot summer's day, Osbert was known to fix a fringed canopy over his lawnmower, although this was more to protect his bald head than to decorate his machine. Besides, the canopy had been specially knitted by Aunt Gardenia Bogey-Mandeville who lived downstairs and ran

Creakie Hall as a hotel. And even though Aunt Gardenia was the sweetest old lady with a voice like a tiny silver bell, no one said *no* to one of her specially knitted covers.

Just at that moment, Osbert Codseye trundled into view on his lawnmower. He swung right around an old oak tree and headed towards the main flower bed.

'Excellent!' chuckled Marmaduke. 'He'll see it any minute!'

'See what?' said Miasma suspiciously. She turned and gave her husband a stern stare. 'Marmaduke! What have you done?'

'Nothing,' replied Marmaduke, fiddling with a dagger hanging from his belt. 'I only planted a flower bed for him.'

'Let me see!' cried Miasma, grabbing the telescope. A close-up of the main flower bed appeared before her. 'Marmaduke!' she exclaimed. 'What lovely black and white tulips and what a pretty skull and crossbones! I'm sure Osbert will be delighted.'

A strange strangled noise floated into the air. It was a cross between a scream and a choke. Osbert Codseye stared, stiff and open-mouthed, while the lawnmower beneath him motored

on towards the flower bed. A single violent spasm shook his body then he slumped forward over the wheel. Miasma watched as a boy and a girl raced across the grass towards him.

Just in time, the boy grabbed the wheel and stopped the lawnmower before it ploughed into the flower bed. A second later, Osbert Codseye tumbled out of the driver's seat and lay in a heap on the grass.

'We'll take him to his shed,' said the girl calmly. 'He'll feel better in the dark.' She had green eyes and a thatch of orange hair. She looked across at the flower bed. 'I like the black and white tulips.'

The boy nodded. 'Brilliant skull and crossbones.'

They bent down and took an arm each. Then they dragged Osbert Codseye across the lawn.

Inside the attic, Miasma clasped her hands together and sighed. 'Marmaduke!' she cried. 'Wouldn't it be fun to see Polly and George again!' Her eyes gleamed. 'I do hope there's another catastrophe at Creakie Hall so we can come down and help out.'

But Marmaduke didn't reply. He was looking through his telescope.

'What is it?' demanded Miasma. 'What can you see?'

She leant out the window and stared at where the telescope was pointing.

A flash of pink glittered between the trees. It was a bright coral pink, not the soft petal pink you might normally associate with spring. As she stared, another pink flash appeared.

'Gimme!' she shouted. And without another word, she snatched the telescope from Marmaduke.

Winding their way slowly down the long drive to Creakie Hall were two huge, bright-pink Rolls Royces. Men holding microphones ran along behind them. Flashbulbs popped. Cameras rolled. Voices rose like squawking seagulls into the quiet spring air.

One woman stood with a microphone in her hand in front

of a camera. She wore a short, scarlet suit with huge gold buttons. Miasma trained the telescope on her face and waited.

Over the years in the attic, Miasma had also taken up various hobbies to pass the time. One of these hobbies had been lip-reading.

The young woman began to speak. These were the words Miasma saw.

'HOLLYWOOD COMES TO CREAKIE HALL!'

'Bogey-baby!' cried Marmaduke. 'What is it?'

Miasma's eyes were tight shut and her hair stuck out all over her head.

For a moment, Miasma didn't speak. Then suddenly she threw her right arm in the air. 'Marmaduke,' she declared, her cat-green eyes glittering in the shadowy attic. 'Marmaduke, I have had a vision.'

'You have?' said Marmaduke.

'I have,' cried Miasma. 'And I have seen a great truth.'

'You have?' said Marmaduke.

'I have,' cried Miasma.

'What is it?' asked Marmaduke, his arms fluttering at his sides.

Miasma grinned her wolfish grin, leapt on to the card table and held both arms out wide. 'It is never too late to get into the movies,' she cried. 'Marmaduke! Our time has come!'

CHAPTER 2

INSIDE THE FIRST Rolls Royce, Chubby Cellophane, Hollywood super-director, spat out a half-chewed smoked salmon sandwich, leaned back on his seat and spilled pink champagne all over the white velvet covers.

In the corner, his assistant sat pressed up against the window, her hands folded tightly in her lap.

'Yeuch!' muttered Chubby, wiping his hands on his assistant's skirt. 'I *hate* sticky stuff.'

He crossed his legs and knocked

over a tin of caviar. Gluey black eggs dripped onto the floor.

Chubby Cellophane turned to the young woman in the corner. 'Um, whatever your name is,' he said, 'make sure the hotel cleans this mess up. I hate *gooey* things too.'

'Yessir,' muttered his assistant, making a note in her notepad. 'Anything else, sir?'

'Yeah,' said Chubby Cellophane,

yawning, 'mind if I call you Thingy-Wotsits? It's sorta easier that way.'

The young woman stiffened. 'Thingy-Wotsits,' she repeated in an icy voice. 'Of course, sir. Anything you want, sir.'

'Good girl, Thingy,' replied Chubby Cellophane, patting his huge, wobbling belly. 'That's why I hired you. I get anything I want.'

Inside the back of the second Rolls Royce, Slick Shivers, Hollywood actor and superstar, ran his hand through his glossy blonde hair and practised smiling in the rear-view mirror. The diamond drilled into a front tooth sparkled in the morning sun.

'Now that's what I call a dazzling smile,' he said to himself with a dazzling smile. 'Whaddya think, Blare?'

Beside him Blare Gemstone, world-famous actress and superstarlet, was peering into the tiny mirror she usually kept glued to the palm of her left hand. There was something wrong with her deep-purple eyes — one of them was light brown. 'I think you're sitting on one of my contact lenses,' she replied in a low, gravelly voice that sounded as if it came from the bottom of a well.

Slick Shivers leapt across the seat as if he'd seen a great, hairy tarantula. 'Ugh!' he cried. He pulled back his lips. 'How *could* you?'

Blare Gemstone picked up the tiny lens and once again became the actress with the incredible purple eyes. 'For the same reason you stuck a lump of glass in your front tooth,'

she replied. 'I wanna be the star in Chubby Cellophane's new movie.'

Slick Shivers absent-mindedly began to suck his thumb. 'Yeah,' he said slowly. 'We sure wanna do better than last time.' He cringed at the memory of their last film.

It had been called *Things from the Swamp*. Slick and Blare had been coated in mud and given slide-on parts. That way you don't have to say much, the director had explained.

Blare Gemstone watched through her purple eyes. She knew what Slick was thinking. 'Never mind *wanna*. We *gotta* do better than last time.' She stuck on a feather-duster-sized false eyelash. 'So remember, if we act like superstars that fat jerk Cellophane'll treat us like superstars and sign us up.'

A sly glint came into Slick Shivers' eyes. 'Yeah,' he said. 'What he don't know won't hurt him.'

'Yeah,' replied Blare Gemstone. 'But it'll hurt us if he finds out.' She stuck on the other feather duster. 'So act like a superstar, right?'

'Right.'

Miasma wasn't the only person who saw the two Rolls Royces. After Polly and George had taken Osbert Codseye to his garden shed and wrapped him up in one of Aunt Gardenia's cosy, knitted survival blankets while he recovered from his shock, they raced round to the front hall.

'Polly! George!' cried Aunt Gardenia in her high, tinkling voice. 'How wonderful to see you! I've almost finished it!'

'Finished what?' asked Polly.

Aunt Gardenia chuckled and pulled at a rope by her side. A huge knitted screen unfurled down the wall.

Polly gasped. It was a picture of a lion standing on his back legs in front of a snow-capped mountain. He held a flaming torch in one paw and banged a gong with his tail. CREAKIE HALL PRESENTS was knitted in rainbow colours over the top.

Aunt Gardenia beamed from ear to ear. 'Do you think he'll like it?' she cried.

Polly and George looked sideways at each other. Aunt Gardenia was obviously over-excited. At times like these, it was always a good idea to stay as calm as possible even though inside they felt as if they were going to explode.

Polly and George took a deep breath, counted to ten, and said as

slowly as they could manage, 'Who is going to like what?'

'Chubby Cellophane, of course,' cried Aunt Gardenia. 'The world-famous Hollywood director. He's making a movie at Creakie Hall!'

Aunt Gardenia's eyes twinkled as if she knew she had been terribly clever. 'Which means, of course,' she explained in a loud whisper, 'after the movie comes out, everyone who's anyone will come and stay at Creakie Hall!'

Aunt Gardenia swept across the room towards the window. 'What's more, Mr Cellophane is bringing two superstars with him!'

'Who?' cried Polly and George jumping up and down with excitement. Movies were their hobby. There was nothing they didn't know about movies.

It was supposed to be Aunt Gardenia's final triumph. She spun like a dancer and threw both arms in the air. 'Blare Gemstone and Slick Shivers!' she cried.

Polly and George looked at each other. They had never heard of Blare Gemstone or Slick Shivers.

'Who are they?' asked George.

But Aunt Gardenia didn't hear him because at that moment two pink Rolls Royces roared through the gates, slid to a stop, and sprayed a wave of gravel against the front of the house.

Polly and George stared in amazement. In front of their eyes, the hotel courtyard was filling up with more cars, more cameras, more reporters and more suitcases than they had ever seen in their lives.

Hollywood had come to Creakie Hall!

CHAPTER 3

FROM THEIR UPSTAIRS attic window, Miasma and Marmaduke had the best view of all. They saw Chubby Cellophane introduce himself to Aunt Gardenia. They saw Blare Gemstone in a tight, sequin dress ooze from the door of her Rolls Royce like a dollop of golden syrup. And they saw Slick Shivers strutting about like a cartoon cowboy.

Miasma and Marmaduke were decidedly over-excited too. Ever since Miasma's vision, they had tried all sorts of parts. Miasma as Maid

Marion, Marmaduke as Robin Hood. Miasma as Lois Lane, Marmaduke as Superman. Miasma as gorgeous lady spy, Marmaduke as James Bond.

'Phew!' gasped Miasma, who had just turned from being a lioness to a mermaid to a princess and back to herself again. 'How about Cinderella? You can be Prince Charming.'

But Marmaduke was being stubborn. He didn't want to be Prince Charming or the Alien from Outer Space or anything else for that matter. Marmaduke only wanted to be one thing – a pirate.

'But, spooky-pet,' cried Miasma, who had turned into Cinderella anyway, 'Chubby Cellophane might not be making a pirate movie. You'll ruin my chances.'

'If Chubby Cellophane isn't making a pirate movie, then he's making a mistake,' roared Marmaduke. He grabbed hold of the chandelier, swung across the room and smashed into the wall.

'Wow!' murmured Miasma, gazing at him with her hands clasped over her exquisitely ragged rag dress. 'That was *beautiful*, bogey-baby.'

There was a tremendous clanking as Marmaduke picked himself up and dusted himself down. 'What's more,' he cried, waving his sword in the air, 'I'm going to tell him so.'

He rested a gloved hand on Miasma's shoulder. 'Come, sweet maid,' he groaned, rubbing his knees with his other hand. 'Throw off those rags and follow your destiny.'

'But I thought I was going with you,' said Miasma.

Marmaduke rolled his eyes. 'You are, spooky-pet, you are,' he muttered.

So Miasma turned into Space Queen from Mars and the two of them disappeared into thin air.

'Champagne, dear lady!' cried Chubby Cellophane, smacking his lips and pumping Aunt Gardenia's hand. 'We must celebrate!'

'Champagne, Mr Cellophane?' replied Aunt Gardenia, a little taken aback.

'Four bottles, at least,' cried Chubby Cellophane. He turned and muttered in Thingy-Wotsits' ear, 'The old bat's deaf. Make a note of that.'

'Four bottles?' cried Aunt Gardenia. This was not what she had expected at all. Coffee was waiting in the dining room and Osbert Codseye had made a plate of tiny iced lawnmower cakes and a selection of gingerbread gardeners.

'Four bottles,' repeated Chubby Cellophane. 'One for me, one for Blare, one for Slick.' He paused as if he was trying to remember something. 'And one for you, of course, dear lady!' He smiled broadly but the smile on his face did not match the look in his eyes.

Aunt Gardenia was totally confused. On the one hand, it seemed terribly rude for someone to arrive and immediately demand champagne – even if they were a Hollywood director. But, then again, what would Aunt Gardenia know? Perhaps that's the way superstars behaved. After all, it was a special occasion. And it wasn't as if money was a problem. Hadn't Mr Cellophane waved his arms around and promised that he would, of course, pay for 'everything, absolutely everything'. Heaven knows, Creakie Hall could never afford to look after such famous people with such fancy tastes!

Aunt Gardenia sighed a little sigh. It was all so exciting! Of course, Chubby Cellophane was right. Champagne was the only thing. A cup of coffee would seem mean and ridiculous.

She looked up and beamed into Chubby Cellophane's rubbery, loose-jawed face. 'A marvellous idea, dear,' she cried. 'How silly of me not to suggest it. Polly! George! Fetch the best glasses and four bottles of champagne.'

As George rushed away, Slick Shivers sidled over to where Polly was standing. 'Hey, kid,' he hissed, 'make sure it's *real* champagne. We only

drink the best, you know.' He flashed his dazzling smile.

Polly stared at the diamond in Slick Shivers' front tooth. Even she could see it was only a piece of glass. A cold tingling feeling passed through her stomach. Something wasn't right about this so-called movie star.

'And get me a round of caviar sandwiches,' added Slick Shivers. 'Mustard and ketchup on the side.'

The cold tingling feeling in Polly's stomach turned into an icy lump. As she raced through the hall and down towards the cellar, she ran through in her mind all the movies she and George had seen together. She searched them for the faces of Blare Gemstone and Slick Shivers.

Slowly but surely, a scene began to take form. Polly shook her head. It couldn't be the right one. But the

scene grew clearer and clearer. By the time she reached the top of the cellar stairs even the name of the movie was sharp and unmistakable. *Things from the Swamp.* Polly let the credits roll in front of her eyes.

Slide-on Parts – Blare Gemstone and Slick Shivers.

Polly's heart went *bang!* in her chest. George! Where was George? She ran down the stairs two at a time and was just about to shout out his name when a gust of icy wind fluttered past her.

'Dahling!' cried Miasma, appearing out of nowhere in her Space Queen from Mars costume. 'How simply fabulous to see you!'

'Flesh'n'bloods, ahoy!' roared Marmaduke, swinging across the cellar on a knotted bedsheet. He dropped lightly to his feet and bowed.

Polly stared open-mouthed.

In front of her, George dropped the tray he was carrying. Four bottles of champagne smashed to bits on the floor.

Miasma leaned forward and smiled her wolfish grin. 'A trifle, earthlings,' she murmured. She waggled her silver fingers in the air.

All the bits of all four bottles of champagne joined up and bounced back onto the tray.

Marmaduke rattled his sword and winked. *Ping! Ping! Ping! Ping!* Four crystal goblets took their places beside each bottle.

As Polly looked at her ghostly ancestors, a huge feeling of relief washed over her. 'Thank goodness, you're here!' she cried. And as much to her own surprise as theirs, indeed for the first time since they had known each other, she hugged them both.

'Gee!' cried Miasma, hugging Polly in return. She looked at Marmaduke, her wolfish grin wider than ever. 'Emotional or what?'

'Heartfelt, honeybunch,' agreed Marmaduke in a choked voice.

Polly smiled shyly and unwrapped herself from Miasma's arms. 'There's something I have to tell you,' she said quietly. 'It's about those movie people. We've got to sort them out before it's too late!'

'What are you talking about?' cried Miasma. 'It's never too late to get into the movies!'

George put down his tray and looked at Polly. '*Things from the Swamp*,' he said quietly.

'What do you mean *Things from the Swamp*?' demanded Miasma. 'I'm a Space Queen from Mars and Marmaduke's a pirate.'

'You don't understand,' said Polly. 'Those movie people are fakes. Blare Gemstone and Slick Shivers aren't superstars. And I'll bet my bottom dollar Chubby Cellophane isn't a big Hollywood director either.'

'Exactly,' said George. He frowned. 'And somehow we've got to convince Aunt Gardenia before they bankrupt Creakie Hall.'

Miasma's vision of fame and glory evaporated. She went green with fury. 'I'll banish them to Planet X!' she cried. 'They shall live out their lives in outer darkness.'

'I'll slice them into tiny pieces and feed them to the sharks,' yelled Marmaduke, waving his sword.

'What sharks?' asked Miasma slowly. 'There aren't any sharks in Bullfrog Lake.'

A wicked gleam came into Marmaduke's eyes.

'Don't you dare!' cried Polly. 'We have to be terribly careful. Aunt Gardenia will be devastated if she finds out she's been hoodwinked by a bunch of cheats and liars.'

'Sharks!' cried Marmaduke again. 'It's the only answer.'

'No sharks,' said George in his most serious voice.

Marmaduke looked sadly at the razor-sharp sword at his waist. 'You're right,' he muttered. 'How about –' And at that moment, he made a great decision.

Quick as a flash, he turned himself into a cowboy. His pirate phase was over.

Marmaduke pulled out a rope and lassoed the ceiling light. 'How about if I tie them up instead.'

'And leave them to roast in the desert sun!' cried Miasma, who had read lots of Westerns over the years. 'Whaddyathink, flesh'n'bloods?'

There was no answer.

This time it was Polly and George who had disappeared.

CHAPTER 4

FIVE DAYS LATER, Polly and George stood in the front hall. Their faces were as long as two wet socks on a washing line. Perhaps it was already too late.

Creakie Hall had been turned upside down. Blare Gemstone had installed herself on the first floor and had ordered a team of hairdressers, make-up artists, manicurists, and a personal gymnasium with two trainers – one for her left leg and one for her right leg.

Slick Shivers had taken over the

next floor and had built a boxing ring and his own movie theatre with indoor jacuzzi and sauna.

Meanwhile, Chubby Cellophane had moved into the main reception room and was on the phone to New York ordering hamburgers to be flown over to make his stars feel at home.

All the while, messengers ran backwards and forwards with crates of champagne and fancy baskets of exotic fruit. There was even an oil drum full of caviar sitting on the doorstep. As Polly watched, twenty-four bottles of ketchup and a huge jar of mustard were plonked down beside it.

'George,' she whispered, 'we must find Aunt Gardenia.'

George jerked his head in the direction of the dining room. He held a finger to his lips and the two of them crept over to the closed door.

On the other side, Chubby Cellophane's voice was low and urgent. 'Look, Harry, we're partners, aren't we? You don't have to worry about the money. The old bat who runs this joint is paying for everything.' He allowed himself a smug snort of a laugh. 'Of course, *she* thinks I'm paying. What was that, Harry?

'Of course, there ain't gonna be no movie, not at this dump anyway. Harry, listen to me, this is just a public-relations exercise.'

'What's a public-relations exercise?' whispered Polly in a trembling voice.

George shook his head.

Chubby Cellophane began talking again. 'Look, Harry, Blare and Slick are superstars. I gotta make sure they think I'm signing them up for a big movie.' He laughed unpleasantly. 'But first I gotta pretend *I'm* a big Hollywood director. Darnnit, Harry, I can't make dog-food commercials for the rest of my life.'

He banged down the phone. A second later, they heard his voice again. 'Is that China? Fantastic! I wanna order two takeaways.'

Polly put her hands over her face and stumbled outside into the warm spring air.

George followed her, his face the colour of candle wax.

They found Aunt Gardenia sitting on a bench in front of Bullfrog Lake talking to Thingy-Wotsits. The strange thing was that the more Aunt Gardenia talked, the more uncomfortable and unhappy Thingy-Wotsits looked.

'Of course, my niece and nephew, Polly and George, are delighted to be in the movie too,' Aunt Gardenia was saying in her silvery voice.

Thingy-Wotsits mumbled something and stared at her feet.

'I can't tell you how pleased I am that Mr Cellophane chose our hotel,' continued Aunt Gardenia. 'Creakie Hall will never be the same again.'

'You can say that again,' said George, coming up behind them.

'In fact, we may never recover,' added Polly, staring at Thingy-Wotsits.

'George! Polly!' cried Aunt Gardenia. 'Come and meet Tallulah Tempest. She's Mr Cellophane's assistant. Such a pretty name, don't you think? And that naughty Mr Cellophane is so busy, he can never remember it.'

Thingy-Wotsits raised her head and smiled at them. 'Hello,' she said quietly. 'I was trying to explain to your Aunt Gardenia about the movie business.' She paused, looking more uncomfortable than ever.

Polly stared at her. Behind her pulled-back, blonde hair and horn-rim glasses, she had the most extraordinary blue eyes. And there was something else. Suddenly, Polly was sure that this young woman knew that Chubby Cellophane was a conman and a liar and she was trying to warn Aunt Gardenia before it was too late.

'Aunt Gardenia doesn't know about public-relations exercises,' muttered Polly angrily. As far as she was concerned, a public-relations exercise was just another word for telling lies.

Thingy-Wotsits blushed. 'I was trying to explain to her,' she said in a miserable voice. 'Really, it's just another word for –'

'Polly dear!' cried Aunt Gardenia, thinking she was helping Thingy-

Wotsits. 'Don't you understand? Everyone knows exercise is important. Why, every day Osbert Codseye and I take a stroll through the maze.' She patted Thingy-Wotsits' knee. 'But I wouldn't recommend it for you, dear,' she added sweetly. 'Some people say it's more like a prison. You should concentrate on your career.'

Tears glistened in Thingy-Wotsits' eyes. 'It was lovely to talk to you,

Aunt Gardenia,' she murmured, 'but I must get back to Mr Cellophane.'

Aunt Gardenia beamed. 'And just you tell him what a brilliant young actress you really are, Tallulah, dear,' she cried. 'Silly to hide candles under covers, you know.' And with that, she got up and bustled over to the main flower bed where Osbert Codseye was standing and wringing his hands.

Thingy-Wotsits smiled sadly and said almost to herself, 'There's no point telling Mr Cellophane. He wouldn't listen.'

'Then why do you work for him?' asked George.

'Because I didn't know that when I started,' replied Thingy-Wotsits. 'And he promised to give me a part in the movies.'

Polly took a deep breath. It was time to find out exactly how much Thingy-Wotsits knew. 'How could Chubby Cellophane give you a part in the movies?' she asked.

Thingy-Wotsits looked surprised. 'Because he's a big Hollywood director, of course.'

Anger flushed Polly's cheeks. 'He's not a big Hollywood director,' she said. 'He makes dog-food commercials.'

Now it was George's turn. 'Blare

Gemstone and Slick Shivers are fakes,' he said furiously. 'The only movie they've ever been in was called *Things from the Swamp*.'

Thingy-Wotsits sat down. For a moment she said nothing. When she looked up, her blue eyes shone with rage. 'Are you sure about this?'

'Positive,' said Polly.

'Then Chubby Cellophane has lied to all of us,' said Thingy-Wotsits in a cold, icy voice.

'So what are we going to do about it?' cried a voice behind them. Marmaduke strode out of the maze wearing fringed buffalo-hide trousers and a huge stetson hat.

'Hang 'em high,' cried Miasma, swaggering along behind him. Miasma was now dressed up as a cowgirl with a mean-looking whip in her right hand.

Suddenly, a new look crossed Thingy-Wotsits' face. She pulled off her glasses and stamped on them. Then she shook out her hair. The look on her face was hard and angry.

Thingy-Wotsits was gone. Tallulah Tempest had taken her place. And Tallulah's time had come.

'I'll help you,' cried Tallulah Tempest, her blue eyes still blazing. 'That fat crook will wish he'd never been born.'

A wide, wicked grin spread across Miasma's face. She turned to Polly. 'Who is your delightful friend, my dear?' she purred. 'I don't think we've been introduced.'

Polly swallowed and turned to Tallulah. 'These are . . . our . . . um . . .' She looked desperately at George.

'Our great aunt and uncle,' said George. 'They're, ah, actors too.'

At that moment, a gleaming red seaplane roared out of the sky, landed on Bullfrog Lake and bounced over the water towards them.

A tubby little man with a bald head jumped out onto the wing and waved frantically. He was wearing a silver raincoat and a pair of wrap-around sunglasses.

'Oh no,' muttered George, 'not another actor!'

Polly stared over the water. Suddenly her face lit up. 'It's not another actor,' she cried. 'It's Barney Loot! Remember? He'll know *exactly* what to do!'

CHAPTER 5

'GRACIOUS!' CRIED AUNT Gardenia as she wandered back to the crowd by the lake. 'What a wonderful reunion!' She beamed at Marmaduke and Miasma. 'And are you still magicians, dears? I'll never forget your last entertainments.'

Miasma grinned from ear to ear. 'We're actors now, Aunt Gardenia,' she said proudly. 'You name it, we can —'

'Do you remember Mr Loot, Aunt Gardenia?' interrupted Polly desperately. 'He stayed with us when Creakie Hall first opened as a hotel.'

'Of course I do,' cried Aunt Gardenia. 'How lovely to see you again.' She patted Barney Loot's hand. 'It was so kind of you to leave us that gold brick. Did you ever make your movie?' She tilted her head to one side. 'What was it about again?'

Barney Loot threw back his head and hooted with laughter. 'A mass

prison breakout that ends happily ever after,' he said. 'Yup! I sure did and I'm as happy as I'll ever be!'

'Splendid!' said Aunt Gardenia. 'We're happy too, you know. A very important Hollywood director is making a movie at Creakie Hall!'

'I know all about it,' replied Barney Loot. He suddenly looked serious. 'I've just been speaking to Polly. She's told me everything.'

Aunt Gardenia clasped her hands and her eyes twinkled. 'It's so exciting,' she laughed. 'I've never met such people before.'

'I have,' said Barney Loot. 'Those kind of people are a special breed.'

'Are they?' cried Aunt Gardenia. 'I'm so glad you told me. I *was* beginning to wonder.' At that moment, she noticed the scarlet seaplane bobbing gently on Bullfrog Lake.

'It's beautiful, isn't it?' murmured Miasma in a suggestive sort of way. She fixed Aunt Gardenia with her cat-green eyes. 'And such fun to fly, I would imagine.'

Aunt Gardenia's eyes twinkled. 'Why, that's just what I was thinking!' she cried.

She paused and drew her eyebrows together in a worried sort of way. 'There is just one thing.'

'What?' cried Barney, Miasma, Marmaduke, Polly, George and Tallulah.

'Do you think Osbert could come too?' whispered Aunt Gardenia. 'You see, he's had this rather . . . ah . . . unexpected surprise and —'

'My pleasure,' cried Barney Loot. He held out the keys. 'It's just like driving a lawnmower.'

A minute later, there was a watery

roar and the red seaplane thundered away across the lake.

'Excellent,' cried Miasma, rubbing her hands. 'Now we can get down to business.'

'Not so fast, spooky-pet,' cried Marmaduke, twirling a six-shooter in his right hand. 'What about the movie Aunt Gardenia's expecting?'

Barney Loot grinned. 'Funny you should mention movies,' he said.

'You see, I just happen to make them myself.'

'Of course,' cried Tallulah Tempest. 'I knew I'd seen you before. You're the President of Goldbrick Productions. You make the world's greatest Westerns.'

'Kind of you to say so, Miss Tempest,' said Barney Loot. 'And I hear you're a terrific actress.'

'An' I can rope a rattler with ma eyes half-shut,' drawled Miasma.

'I'm sure you can, dear lady,' said Barney Loot, smoothly. 'In fact, it seems to me as if we have the makings of an entire cast right here.'

'We do?' cried Polly in amazement.

'We do,' replied Barney Loot. 'There's only one problem.'

'What's that?' said Miasma.

Barney Loot pulled a face. 'You need all kinds of equipment to make a movie and we don't have a lot of time!'

'That's not a problem!' cried Miasma. She gave a low whistle. Six jet-black horses trotted out of the maze towards them.

'The equipment's waiting!' yelled Miasma, vaulting on to the nearest horse. 'Let's go!'

'Yeuch!' spluttered Slick Shivers. 'Do we *have* to wash our teeth in champagne?'

'Of course we do,' replied Blare Gemstone, gargling a mouthful of Moët Chandon Extra-Dry-and-Incredibly-Expensive. 'Besides, it gets rid of the taste of those yucky takeaways.' She spat out a stream of bubbles and watched them disappear into the plug hole.

'Blare,' whined Slick Shivers, 'do you think this is working? I mean, Chubby Cellophane hasn't even *mentioned* the movie yet and we've been here for almost a week.'

Blare Gemstone outlined her hard, red mouth with lipstick so that it was even harder and redder. 'I got an idea,' she said. 'Why don't we pretend another director has offered us starring roles in another movie?'

Her eyes gleamed as the plan took shape. 'We'll tell Chubby Cellophane it's now or never.'

'But we don't know any other directors,' said Slick Shivers in a sulky voice.

'Of course we do,' snarled Blare. She picked a well-thumbed copy of *We Done Good – A Guide to Mega Moguls*. Then she closed her eyes and threw the magazine in the air. Pages fluttered open as it landed on the floor.

Slick Shivers bent down and looked at the open page.

'Who is it?' asked Blare Gemstone.

'Barney Loot,' muttered Slick Shivers. 'Ever heard of him?'

'Sure have,' replied Blare with a smirk. 'I once played a dead Indian in one of his Westerns.' She strode to the door. 'Come on, sissy. Barney

Loot's just offered us a million dollars. Got it?'

Slick Shivers flicked a noodle off the front of his brand-new, white leather jacket. Then he checked out his front tooth in the bathroom mirror.

'Got it,' he said with a dazzling smile.

CHAPTER 6

'SO THAT'S THE situation, dahling,' murmured Blare Gemstone. She smiled her warmest smile. 'It's now or never, as they say.'

'Yeah,' agreed Slick Shivers. 'We're real sorry to rush ya but a million dollars is a million dollars.'

'Yeah,' said Blare. She slid off the chair and crossed the room like a limbo dancer going forwards. 'Come on, Slick. Let's leave Mr Cellophane to think things over. 'Sides, I wan' another of them yummy champagne cocktails.'

'Anything you say, princess,' said Slick Shivers in a gruff voice.

The door closed behind them and Chubby Cellophane sat on his own in the middle of a sea of stale takeaways.

He covered his face with his sweaty, pudgy hands. How could they do this to him? How could they be so greedy? After all he'd done for them. Where was their loyalty? Where was their shame? And for that matter, where was what's her name, Thingy-Wotsits? Chubby Cellophane kicked over a tower of cardboard cups. The place was a mess and Chubby Cellophane hated a mess. It stopped him thinking straight.

There was a knock at the door. Chubby Cellophane jumped into his chair and put his legs up on the desk. That must be her. About time too.

'Yeah,' he said.

'Dahling!' cried Miasma, sweeping into the room. She was dressed in a swirling, sequined gown edged in turquoise ostrich feathers. She touched his cheek with an icy hand.

Chubby Cellophane nearly jumped out of his chair. 'Who are you?' he cried.

'Me?' cried Miasma. 'I guess you could call me an *old* friend.' She laughed a hollow laugh that sounded like an echo in a vault and closed her cold fingers around his wrist. 'An old friend of Aunt Gardenia's, that is.'

'What do you want?' said Chubby Cellophane in a trembling voice. There was something very peculiar about this woman.

Miasma grinned her wolfish grin. 'You are Chubby Cellophane?' she murmured. 'The *famous* Hollywood director?'

Chubby began to relax. 'Of course I am,' he said in a nasty voice. 'And I'm very busy. What do you want?'

'To show you something special,' cried Miasma. 'Come along! *Everyone's* waiting for you.'

And before Chubby Cellophane could pull back she dragged him into the hall and out onto the front steps.

Chubby Cellophane's jaw dropped open. He was standing at one end of a dusty street somewhere in Texas around the turn of the century. Cowboys on horses trotted past. Wagons loaded with sacks of flour and bales of cloth trundled over to the general store. Halfway down the street, the double doors of a saloon bar swung open.

Tallulah Tempest stepped out. She wore high-heeled cowboy boots and a black leather skirt. She looked about as friendly as a rattle snake.

'Hello, Mr Cellophane,' she said in

a dangerous voice. 'Reckon you don't remember me.'

Chubby Cellophane's rubbery face went the colour of a cardboard cup. His mouth went up and down but no sound came out.

Miasma's icy hand gripped tighter. 'This way, dahling,' she cried. She pushed Chubby Cellophane down the street and through the double doors into a small movie theatre.

'Chubby! Sweetheart!' cried Blare Gemstone, giving him her widest smile and wrapping her arms around him like a hungry python. 'Why didn't you tell me you were making a Western?' She fixed him with her incredible purple eyes. 'Westerns happen to be my speciality. I starred in Barney Loot's latest.'

'That so?' said Barney Loot quietly.

Blare Gemstone turned, saw a

tubby little man and went back to Chubby Cellophane. 'Yeah, me an' Barney are real pals.' She laughed confidentially. 'Couldn't direct his way out of a paper bag, of course. Not like you, Chubby.'

Chubby Cellophane stared at the tubby little man and recognised him immediately. This time a strangled noise came from the back of his throat.

'Yeah,' drawled Slick Shivers. 'It was Blare's acting that saved the movie.' He flashed his dazzling smile. 'Funny thing. Exactly the same thing happened to me in *my* last movie.'

'That so?' said Barney Loot again.

'Ladies and gentlemen!' cried Marmaduke, who looked splendid in a white tail coat. 'Take your seats. The show is about to begin.'

Chubby Cellophane began to

make a low moaning noise as he was half carried, half dragged to the front row. He knew in his bones something terrible was about to happen.

The lights dimmed and a picture of a shop window came up on the screen. In the middle of the window on a velvet-covered table stood a tin of dog food. Over the top, children sang in high sugary voices, 'How much is that dog food in the window?'

The entire scene lasted for three seconds. At the end came the words: *Written, directed and produced by Chubby Cellophane.*

No one spoke.

Another picture came up on the screen. '*Things from the Swamp.* Slide-on parts: Blare Gemstone and Slick Shivers.' The scene showed a swamp covered in green slime. Two muddy lumps could be seen at the edge.

But they weren't just lumps. They had eyes.

Slowly the two lumps slid into the swamp and sunk below the green slime. Then came two words: *The End*.

Chubby Cellophane stared at the screen as if all his worst nightmares had come at once.

Blare Gemstone looked as if she had been turned to stone.

'It's all *her* fault,' screamed Slick Shivers, jamming his thumb in his mouth. 'It wath her idthea in the firthst plathe.'

'You little *creep*!' snarled Blare Gemstone. 'You and your fake glass tooth.'

Slick Shivers pulled out his thumb. 'You and your fake purple eyes!' he screamed. He turned to Chubby Cellophane who sat cowering in his chair with his hands over his head. 'And *you're* the biggest fake of all! Dog-food commercials! Huh, you're no better than dog food yourself!'

'Excellent!' cried Miasma, rubbing her silver hands and grinning. 'Now we *all* know who we are, don't we?'

'And *now* we have two choices,' said Barney Loot in a low, angry voice. 'You work for me for free and I will use your wages to pay back Aunt Gardenia.' He paused and fixed them all with a terrible stare. 'Or else everyone who's anyone will know all about your nasty lies and you'll never work again.'

Chubby Cellophane looked sideways at Slick Shivers who looked sideways at Blare Gemstone.

'So what do you want us to do?' said Blare Gemstone in a sulky voice.

'Make tea,' cried Miasma, looking at Chubby Cellophane.

'Cut sandwiches,' said Marmaduke, looking at Slick Shivers.

'And you can look after Miss Tempest's wardrobe,' said Barney Loot, glaring at Blare Gemstone.

'How long will Aunt Gardenia and Osbert Codseye be away?' asked Polly nervously.

Miasma looked at Barney Loot. 'How long will it take?' she asked, raising her eyebrows in a mischievous way.

'A few weeks,' said Barney Loot, 'now that we have all the equipment.'

Miasma beamed and patted Polly on the shoulder. 'Don't worry, dear,' she said. 'Aunt Gardenia will be away for a few weeks.'

'Polly! George!' cried Aunt Gardenia. 'We're back!'

Polly and George ran down the front stairs. Aunt Gardenia looked tanned and fit after her trip across the Pacific Ocean. She threw down her bag and waved a newspaper in the air. 'Look!' she cried. 'I found this at the airport in Los Angeles!'

Polly and George gasped. There was a huge picture of Tallulah

Tempest and Barney Loot standing in front of an enormous movie theatre. Underneath were the words: 'A Star is Born! Blonde-haired bombshell Tallulah Tempest has shot to fame in Barney Loot's new Western *Crackdown at Creakie Hall*. Miss Tempest was modest about her new-found fame. "I couldn't have done it without the help and support of all my friends, especially Polly and George and Miasma and Marmaduke. And, of course, Barney Loot. Also, I would like to thank Chubby for his tea, Slick for his sandwiches and Blare for her ironing. But most of all I would like to thank Aunt Gardenia because Creakie Hall is the best hotel in the world!" '

'So you see, dears,' declared Aunt Gardenia in a voice like a tiny silver bell. 'Things have a way of working

out even if I'm not here. Isn't that wonderful?'

Outside there was a throaty roar as the seaplane throttled up.

'Aunt Gardenia,' said Polly slowly, 'you're not going off again, are you?'

'Just to the Amazon, dear,' replied Aunt Gardenia. 'We won't be long.' She giggled and tucked a wisp of silver hair under her flying helmet. 'It's funny, but ever since Hollywood came to Creakie Hall, I feel a bit like a star myself!'

Polly grinned and kissed her aunt goodbye.

'You are a star, Aunt Gardenia,' said George.

As the gleaming red seaplane roared away into the sky, George and Polly turned and walked back up the front steps into the hall.

The portraits of Miasma and Marmaduke Bogey-Mandeville hung in front of them.

'George!' cried Polly. 'Look!'

For a moment neither of them spoke, then they both fell about laughing.

Miasma and Marmaduke were wearing sunglasses!